D1015679

WITHDRAWN

3.4

The Cam Jansen Series

Cam Jansen and the Mystery of the Stolen Diamonds
Cam Jansen and the Mystery of the U.F.O.
Cam Jansen and the Mystery of the Dinosaur Bones
Cam Jansen and the Mystery of the Television Dog
Cam Jansen and the Mystery of the Gold Coins
Cam Jansen and the Mystery of the Babe Ruth Baseball
Cam Jansen and the Mystery of the Circus Clown
Cam Jansen and the Mystery of the Monster Movie
Cam Jansen and the Mystery of the Carnival Prize
Cam Jansen and the Mystery at the Monkey House
Cam Jansen and the Mystery of the Stolen Corn Popper
Cam Jansen and the Mystery of Flight 54
Cam Jansen and the Mystery at the Haunted House
Cam Jansen and the Chocolate Fudge Mystery
Cam Jansen and the Triceratops Pops Mystery
Cam Jansen and the Ghostly Mystery
Cam Jansen and the Scary Snake Mystery
Cam Jansen and the Catnapping Mystery
Cam Jansen and the Barking Treasure Mystery
Cam Jansen and the Birthday Mystery
Cam Jansen and the School Play Mystery
Cam Jansen and the First Day of School Mystery
Cam Jansen and the Tennis Trophy Mystery
Cam Jansen and the Snowy Day Mystery
Cam Jansen and the Valentine Baby Mystery—25th Anniversary Special
Cam Jansen and the Secret Service Mystery
Cam Jansen and the Summer Camp Mysteries—A Super Special
Cam Jansen and the Mystery Writer Mystery
Cam Jansen and the Green School Mystery
Cam Jansen and the Sports Day Mysteries—A Super Special
Cam Jansen and the Basketball Mystery

DON'T FORGET ABOUT THE YOUNG CAM JANSEN
SERIES FOR YOUNGER READERS!

Cam Jansen

and the
Wedding Cake
Mystery

David A. Adler

illustrated by
Joy Allen

VIKING
An Imprint of Penguin Group (USA) Inc.

VIKING
Published by Penguin Group
Penguin Young Readers Group, 345 Hudson Street,
New York, New York 10014, U.S.A.
Penguin Group (Canada), 90 Eglinton Avenue East, Suite 700, Toronto, Ontario,
Canada M4P 2Y3 (a division of Pearson Penguin Canada Inc.)
Penguin Books Ltd, 80 Strand, London WC2R 0RL, England
Penguin Ireland, 25 St Stephen's Green, Dublin 2, Ireland
(a division of Penguin Books Ltd)
Penguin Group (Australia), 250 Camberwell Road, Camberwell, Victoria 3124,
Australia (a division of Pearson Australia Group Pty Ltd)
Penguin Books India Pvt Ltd, 11 Community Centre,
Panchsheel Park, New Delhi – 110 017, India
Penguin Group (NZ), 67 Apollo Drive, Rosedale, North Shore 0632, New Zealand
(a division of Pearson New Zealand Ltd.)
Penguin Books (South Africa) (Pty) Ltd, 24 Sturdee Avenue,
Rosebank, Johannesburg 2196, South Africa

Penguin Books Ltd, Registered Offices: 80 Strand,
London WC2R 0RL, England

First published in 2010 by Viking, a division of
Penguin Young Readers Group

1 3 5 7 9 10 8 6 4 2

Text copyright © David Adler, 2010
Illustrations copyright © Penguin Young Readers Group, 2010
All rights reserved

LIBRARY OF CONGRESS CATALOGING-IN-PUBLICATION DATA
Adler, David A.
Cam Jansen and the wedding cake mystery / by David Adler ;
illustrated by Joy Allen.
p. cm.— (Cam Jansen ; [30])
Summary: When Cam and her father go to a talent show at the
local senior center, Cam's help is needed to find out
who stole a wedding cake from the delivery truck.
ISBN 978-0-670-06295-9 (hardcover)
[1. Talent shows—Fiction. 2. Stealing—Fiction.
3. Mystery and detective stories.] I. Allen, Joy, ill. II. Title.
PZ7.A2615Caw 2010
[Fic]—dc22
2009048129

Printed in China
Set in New Baskerville

Chapter One

"Hey," Danny said. "What color is a hiccup?"

"That riddle is just silly," Beth told him. "I hope you won't tell it at the talent show. And you always talk too fast when you tell your jokes."

"Fast talking makes my jokes even funnier."

Eric said, "Beth and I will juggle. That's not silly."

"And I'll do memory tricks," Cam Jansen said.

Mr. Jansen was driving everyone to the senior center. Cam was in the front seat of the car, next to her father. Her friends Eric, Danny, and Beth were in the backseat.

Cam and her father help out at the senior center. This year they helped plan the Fall party and talent show. Cam asked her friends to be in the show. This was Eric, Danny, and Beth's first visit to the senior center.

"So, what color is a hiccup?" Danny asked again.

Mr. Jansen stopped the car. He waited for the traffic light to change to green.

"How could we know the answer to that?" Mr. Jansen asked Danny. "We've heard hiccups, but we've never seen one."

"It's burple," Danny said, and laughed. "A hiccup is burple."

The light changed to green. Mr. Jansen turned onto a quiet street with large old houses and big front lawns.

"It's funny," Danny said. "A hiccup is like a burp and 'burple' sounds like 'purple.' So a hiccup is burple."

"It's silly," Beth told him.

Mr. Jansen parked his car in front of the senior center. He parked between a blue truck and a yellow truck. Ken's Bake Shop was printed on the side of the blue truck parked in front. Mr. Fancy Fix-It was printed on the side of the yellow truck.

"Look," Cam said, and pointed. "Lucy Lane is taking pictures."

"Lucy Lane is a photographer," Mr. Jansen told Cam's friends. "She will make lots of copies of the pictures. Then Cam and I will help the seniors send them with holiday cards to their friends and family."

Cam and the others got out of the car. They hurried up the front walk.

"Take my picture," Danny said to Lucy Lane.

Lucy Lane was standing just a few feet from an old man with a white mustache.

"I will," she told him. "But first I'm taking Bob's picture."

"Everybody calls me 'Old Bob,'" the old man said. "I own a bookshop. I was on my way into the center when this nice woman said she'd take my picture."

"Smile," Lucy Lane told Old Bob.

He smiled and she took his picture.

Then she turned to Cam and the others.

"Smile, everyone."

Mr. Jansen, Cam, Eric, and Beth smiled. Danny stuck out his tongue. Lucy Lane took their picture.

Cam looked at Lucy Lane and said, "Smile, please."

Lucy Lane put her digital camera down. She pushed her hair back and smiled.

Cam blinked her eyes and said, *"Click!"*

"Cam, take my picture, too," Danny said.

Danny stuck his tongue out.

Cam looked at Danny, blinked her eyes and said, *"Click!"*

Lucy Lane held up her camera. "Here, take a look," she said. Danny and the others looked at the picture on the small screen on the back of her camera.

"I'm sorry," Cam said. "You can't look at the pictures I took. Only I can see them. They're all up here," she said, and pointed to her head.

Cam has an amazing memory. It's as if she has a camera in her head and pictures there of everything she's seen. When she wants to remember something, Cam just looks at the pictures she has in her head. Cam says *"Click!"* is the sound her mental camera makes when it takes a picture.

"Let's go inside," Mr. Jansen said. "It's almost time for the talent show to begin."

Mr. Jansen, Cam and her friends, Lucy Lane, and Old Bob all went into the building.

"Hello! Hello!" a young woman in a long red dress said to Eric, Beth, and Danny. "I'm Judy."

Cam whispered to Eric, "She's the director of the senior center."

"Thank you for helping," Judy told Mr. Jansen, Cam, and her friends. "The main hall is ready. The lights and microphone are set. It's almost time to start."

Mr. Jansen, Cam, and the others followed her into a large room. Lots of chairs were set up in rows. They all faced a small stage. People were standing by tables on the side of the room. Many of the people held canes. Some had walkers. On the tables were trays of cakes, cookies, and fruit. There were also pitchers of water and ice tea.

"Please, find seats," Judy told the seniors. "You can eat later. The show is about to begin."

Chapter Two

Mr. Jansen stood by the microphone.

Cam and her friends sat in the first row of seats facing the stage. Lucy Lane and a man wearing a white apron sat behind them.

"This is Ken," Lucy Lane told Cam and her friends. "He baked the cakes and cookies for the party."

Mr. Jansen waited while the seniors went to their seats.

"That reminds me," Danny whispered. "I'm hungry."

"You just want some cookies," Beth said.

"I don't just want *some* cookies," Danny

whispered. "I want lots of cookies and lots of cake."

Mr. Jansen held the microphone. When everyone was seated he said, "Good morning. Welcome to the Fall party and talent show. Our show begins with jokes. Here is the very funny Danny Pace."

Mr. Jansen gave Danny the microphone. Danny bowed and everyone applauded.

"Listen to this," Danny said, really fast. "I told my teacher to please not punish me for something I didn't do. She said she wouldn't. Then I told her I didn't do my homework."

No one laughed.

"I built a dog house and hammered a nail. Wow! That hurt! It was my fingernail."

Danny waited. But again, no one laughed.

"Then I dropped the hammer on my toe and do you know what I did? I called a tow truck."

This time Danny didn't wait for people to laugh. He quickly told another joke.

"I dropped the hammer on a leopard. Wow! That hit the spot! And I once heard a singing cow. It made beautiful moo-sic."

"His jokes aren't funny," Ken the baker whispered to Lucy Lane.

"And he talks so fast," Lucy said.

Mr. Jansen got on the stage.

"Thank you. Thank you," Mr. Jansen said.

"No, wait. I have more jokes. Do you

know what's cold and white and flies up and down and up and down? It's a mixed-up snowflake."

Mr. Jansen took the microphone from Danny.

"Thank you, Danny Pace," he said.

Cam, Eric, Beth, and a few other people applauded.

"Now," Mr. Jansen told the seniors, "we'll see some memory magic."

Cam got up on stage and stood next to her father.

"Here is my daughter Jennifer Jansen, the girl with the amazing photographic memory."

Jennifer is Cam's real first name. But when people found out about her great memory, they started calling her "The Camera." Soon "The Camera" became just "Cam."

Cam bowed and people applauded.

"Please, come up here," Mr. Jansen said to Lucy Lane and Ken the baker.

When they were onstage, Lucy Lane whispered to Mr. Jansen, "We can't stay very long. We're going to a wedding."

Cam looked at Lucy and Ken. She closed her eyes and said, *"Click!"*

Cam turned and faced the wall behind the stage.

"What color is Lucy's shirt?" Mr. Jansen asked.

"It's blue," Cam answered.

Cam's eyes were still closed. She was still facing the wall.

Cam said, "There are small white flowers on Lucy's shirt. In the middle of each flower is a red dot. And there are ten buttons down the front of her shirt."

Lucy pointed to each of her buttons as she counted them out loud. Cam was right. There were ten.

"She's amazing," Ken said.

Old Bob stood and called out, "What about me? You saw me outside when Lucy took my picture."

"You have a white mustache," Cam said with her eyes still closed.

"What about my shirt?"

"Your shirt is white with green stripes. You have two pens in your shirt pocket. You're wearing black pants and white sneakers."

"Wow!" Bob said. "She really does have a great memory."

Cam opened her eyes. She turned and bowed.

People cheered and applauded.

Lucy Lane whispered to Mr. Jansen, "We really have to go."

"Let's thank Lucy, who took your photographs, and Ken, who baked all the cookies and cakes," Mr. Jansen said. "The photos and cakes are their gifts to the center."

The people in the audience applauded some more. Then Lucy Lane and Ken left the room.

"Now," Mr. Jansen said into the microphone, "here are two great jugglers, Eric Shelton and Beth Kane."

Eric and Beth walked onto the stage. Each held two red rubber balls. They stood beside the microphone and bowed. Then they stepped to the front of the stage several feet apart and faced each other.

Eric threw a ball to Beth. At the very same moment, Beth threw a ball to Eric.

Just then Lucy and Ken hurried back into the room. They rushed down the aisle. Eric

and Beth turned to look at Lucy and Ken,
and the two balls bounced off the stage.

"I can't find my keys," Ken told Mr. Jansen.
"On the way out I reached into my pocket
and the keys to my truck were gone!"

Chapter Three

"That's terrible," Mr. Jansen said.

"It's worse than terrible," Lucy Lane said. "The wedding is in three hours, and we have to get there. Ken baked pastries, cookies, and a cake for the wedding and I'm taking pictures."

"Hey," Old Bob said. "Who stole the keys? That's a mystery. I love mysteries."

"I have my car here," Mr. Jansen told Lucy and Ken. "I can drive you to the wedding."

Ken shook his head.

"My cake is in the truck. If I can't get into my truck, I can't deliver the cake."

"I read lots of mysteries," Bob said. "And

do you know what? I always solve the mystery before the end of the book."

"Cam Jansen doesn't solve mysteries in a book," Eric said. "She solves real mysteries."

Bob said, "I think someone reached into Ken's pocket and stole his keys."

Cam went to the window and looked out.

"The truck is still here," Cam said. "If someone stole the keys, he would have taken the truck. I think Ken just misplaced his keys."

Lucy told Ken to check his pockets.

"I'm right-handed," Ken said, "so my keys are always in this pocket."

Ken reached into his right pants pocket.

"Nothing!"

He reached into the pocket on the left side of his pants.

"No keys."

"You drove here," Eric said. "You had your keys then."

"You brought trays of cookies and cakes in here," Lucy said. "You used your keys to unlock the back of the truck."

"Yes, I did. Maybe I dropped the keys on the walk."

Lucy and Ken left the main hall of the senior center. Then they left the building. Cam stood by the window. She watched Lucy and Ken walk slowly down the front walk looking for Ken's keys.

"Let's get back to our show," Mr. Jansen said into the microphone. "Here again are two great jugglers, Eric Shelton and Beth Kane."

"Hurry," Eric whispered to Beth, "before something else happens."

They started juggling.

"Ken found his keys," Cam called from the window. "He left them in the back door of his truck."

Eric caught the first ball Beth had thrown. He quickly threw it back to Beth. She caught the ball Eric had thrown and quickly threw it back to him.

Bob joined Cam by the window.

"Look," Bob said. "Ken is opening the back of his truck."

Eric and Beth kept juggling. But many of the people in the audience were not watching them. They were waiting to hear what Cam and Bob would say next.

"Lucy and Ken look upset," Bob said. "Now they're coming back."

Eric and Beth stopped juggling.

Lucy and Ken hurried into the main hall.

"I found my keys, but the pastries, cookies, and cake are gone," Ken said. "Someone stole everything I baked for the wedding."

Chapter Four

"I baked all week," Ken said. He sadly shook his head. "The wedding is in three hours. I don't have time to bake all those desserts again."

Mr. Jansen looked at the many trays of cookies and cakes on the tables. "You could take the cakes you gave us to the wedding."

Ken shook his head.

"Thank you, but they wouldn't be nearly enough," Ken said. "And what about the wedding cake? The bride and groom wanted a tall, beautiful wedding cake, and that's what I baked."

Bob turned to Cam. "This is exciting," he

said. "We have just three hours to find the cake."

Judy, the director of the senior center, hurried to the front of the room.

"I just called the police," she said. "They'll be here soon."

"I'm going outside," Bob said. "Maybe this girl with the amazing memory and I can solve the wedding cake mystery before the police even get here."

Bob quickly left the room. Judy, Ken, and Lucy followed him.

"A real mystery!" an old woman with curly

white hair said. "This is the best party we've ever had."

She went outside, too. Lots of seniors followed her.

"Let's go," Danny said.

Cam and her friends followed Mr. Jansen past the tables with the cookies, cakes, and drinks.

Danny took a few large chocolate chip cookies off a tray. He put one in each of his front and back pants pockets. Then he took a large oatmeal raisin cookie and bit into it.

"Ghim ghakigh thum gnow," he whispered to Beth.

"What?"

Danny swallowed.

"I'm taking cookies now," he whispered. "I'm taking the good stuff before Cam's father gives it all to Ken for the wedding."

"Look at all the people around Ken's truck," Eric said to Cam once they were outside. "We won't be able to get close enough to find clues."

Mr. Jansen, Danny, and Beth walked ahead.

Cam and Eric stopped by the entrance to the senior center.

Cam looked at the people crowded around Ken's truck and her father's car. She blinked her eyes and said, "*Click!*"

"Did you see something? Did you find a clue?" Eric asked. "Can you solve the mystery?"

"I see lots of things," Cam answered. "But I don't know who stole the cakes."

Cam and Eric walked toward the truck.

"There you are," Bob called. "I found clues."

Bob unfolded a small piece of paper.

Eric looked at the paper.

"It says 'milk, juice, cereal, bread, and carrots,'" Eric said. "It's a shopping list."

"Don't read the paper! Look at the broken cookie and cookie crumbs on the paper. I found them near the truck. And there are lots more. Whoever stole the wedding cake and cookies opened those big doors at the back of the truck and took them out."

"I bet he took lots of things all at once," Eric said. "That's why he dropped the cookies."

A police car drove up. It parked behind Mr. Jansen's car. Two officers got out, a tall woman and a not-so-tall man.

"I know them," Cam said. "They came to our school. They're Officers Davis and Oppen."

Everyone gathered around the two police officers.

Ken told the officers, "I left my keys in the back door lock. Later, when I found my keys and opened the doors, the cake, pastries, and cookies were gone."

Officer Davis said, "You shouldn't have left your keys in the door."

"Yes, I know," Ken said.

"Look what I found," Bob said. He showed the officers his collection of cookie crumbs. "It's a clue."

"Hey," Officer Oppen said to Cam. "Aren't you the girl with the 'click, click' memory?"

"Yes," Cam said. "I say *'Click!'* when I want to remember something."

"She has an amazing memory," Eric told

the police officers. "She uses it to solve mysteries. I bet she'll remember something that will help you find the missing cake and cookies."

"I hope she remembers something soon," Ken said.

"She's not the only smart one," Danny told the police officers. "I'm smart, too. And I just saw something that I think will help. I may even know where to find the cake."

Chapter Five

"Someone saw the keys in the lock," Danny said. "He opened the truck and took the cookies, cake, and pastries. Now who could have seen the keys?"

Danny looked at the two police officers. He looked at the many people who had gathered around them.

"This is like school," the old woman with curly white hair whispered. "That boy is the teacher and he's giving us a test."

"I don't like tests," another woman whispered back.

Danny waited.

"Well," Officer Davis asked him. "Are you going to tell us?"

Danny pointed to the house next to the senior center.

"Do you see that big front window? Someone in that house looked out and saw the keys. He opened the truck and stole the cakes."

"I don't think so," Beth said. "A big front window doesn't mean someone is a thief."

"Oh, yeah?" Danny said. "I bet right now someone is sitting in that house and eating

wedding cake. I bet he has lots of white icing all over his face and shirt."

"I could knock on the door," Officer Oppen said. "Maybe whoever lives there looked out the window and saw something that will help us."

"Can I go with you?" Bob asked.

Officer Oppen turned and looked at Bob.

"I'll be quiet," Bob said. "I just want to see how a smart police officer solves a mystery."

"Okay," Officer Oppen said. "You can come along."

"I'm coming, too," Danny and Beth said.

"We're all going," Mr. Jansen said.

"Not me," Officer Davis said. "I'm staying here with the baker and his friend. I need to fill out a report, and I still have some questions."

"The police are just knocking on doors and asking questions," the woman with curly white hair said. "Now this is not so exciting. I'm going inside."

"Me, too," her friend said. "I'm tired. I need to sit down."

Most of the seniors went back to the center. Judy, the director of the center, followed them.

Officer Oppen, Danny, Beth, Mr. Jansen, and Bob walked up the front path of the house next to the senior center. They stood on the small porch. Officer Oppen rang the bell. In the middle of the door was a small window. Behind the window was a curtain.

Officer Oppen waited.

Cam and Eric stood in the middle of the walk. Cam looked through the large front window. She watched an old woman slowly get out of a chair by the window. The woman took a cane and walked toward the front door.

The woman pulled aside the curtain and looked out. Then she opened the door.

"Good morning," the woman said to Officer Oppen.

"We're looking for a wedding cake," Danny said. "We're looking for lots of pastries and cookies, too."

The woman slowly shook her head.

"I'm sorry," she said. "I don't have any

cake. My doctor told me not to eat anything sweet."

"Were you home all morning?" Officer Oppen asked. "Did you look outside?"

"I'm always home," the woman answered. "I sit in that big chair by the window and read."

"Did you see anyone by that truck?" Officer Oppen asked.

"Which truck?" the woman asked.

Officer Oppen pointed to Ken's large blue truck.

The woman looked beyond Officer Oppen and the others.

"I see people there now," she said. "But I didn't see anyone there before. I looked out a few times, but mostly I was reading. I was also sleeping. That chair is really comfortable."

"Thank you," Officer Oppen said.

The woman smiled. Then she closed her door. Cam looked through the large front window. She watched the old woman return to her chair

"Did you hear what she said?" Cam whispered to Eric.

"Yes. She said she doesn't eat cake. She also said she falls asleep in her chair."

"Not that," Cam said. "She said she looked out a few times so she saw Ken's truck. But first she asked, 'Which truck?' because there were two. Don't you remember? Dad parked between them. Whoever was in the other truck must have seen the keys Ken left in the back door."

Officer Oppen and the others walked to the next house.

Cam was still standing on the front walk.

"Aren't we going?" Eric asked.

"Just a minute," Cam answered.

She closed her eyes and said, *"Click!"*

She said, *"Click!"* again.

"What are you looking at?" Eric asked.

"I'm trying to remember everything I've seen since we came here. But it doesn't help."

Cam opened her eyes.

"I keep thinking we're missing something."

Eric said, "Let's go. Officer Oppen is at the next house. Maybe the neighbor saw something."

Cam and Eric went next door. They watched Officer Oppen ring the doorbell.

He waited.

He rang the doorbell again and waited.

"I guess no one is home," he said.

"Let's go across the street," Danny said. "Let's check with those people."

Beth told Danny, "We can't bother everyone on the block."

"You're right. We can't," Danny said. "But Officer Oppen can. He's the police."

Officer Oppen said, "It would really help if one of the neighbors saw something. I'm going to ring some more doorbells."

"We'll all go with you," Bob said.

Cam and Eric watched them walk toward the corner.

"Aren't we going?" Eric asked.

"Come on," Mr. Jansen called. "Stay with us."

Cam and Eric followed Officer Oppen and the others.

"Crumbs, keys, cake," Cam said to herself as she walked. "What clue am I missing?"

Chapter Six

"It's important to cross at the corner," Officer Oppen said, "not in the middle of the street."

Officer Oppen and everyone with him walked to the end of the block. They looked both ways to be sure no cars were coming. Then they crossed the street.

"We'll start with the red brick house in the middle of the block," Officer Oppen said.

The brick house was directly opposite Ken's truck.

"Hey, I have a question," Danny said. "It's about wedding cake. What's the best thing to put in one?"

Officer Oppen knocked on the door.

"I also have a question," Eric said. "If someone saw the cake being stolen, why would he wait for Officer Oppen to knock on his door? Wouldn't he call the police?"

"Maybe not," Mr. Jansen said. "If he just saw someone take the cake from Ken's truck, he might not have known it was being stolen."

Officer Oppen knocked on the door again.

"The best thing to put into a wedding cake is your teeth," Danny said.

Danny laughed.

The door opened.

A young man wearing a bathrobe stood there. He looked at the Officer Oppen and all the people with him.

"Did I do something wrong?"

"No. I just want to know if you saw anyone take pastries, cookies, and a wedding cake out of the truck across the street."

The young man looked across the street at Ken's truck. Cam turned and looked, too.

"I didn't see anyone take anything," the young man said. "I just woke up."

"Thank you," Officer Oppen said.

"Look," Cam whispered. "From here I can only see the truck. I can't see Officer Davis, Ken, or Lucy Lane."

"They must be on the other side of the truck," Eric told her. "That's why you can't see them. It's a tall truck."

Mr. Jansen turned and looked across the street.

"Ken needs a tall truck," he told Cam. "That's because wedding cakes have lots of layers. They can be very high."

"That's it!" Cam said. "That's the clue I was missing."

She told her dad she was crossing the street.

"I need to check one of the clues. I may know who stole the pastries and cake."

"I'll go with you," her dad and Eric said.

They walked to the corner. They waited as two cars went past.

"Did you see those cars?" Cam asked.

"Of course I saw them," Eric answered. "That's why I stop and look before I cross the street. I look for cars."

"Yes," Cam said. "But none of the people in those cars could have stolen the wedding cake."

"Of course those people could not have taken the cake," Cam's dad said. "The cake is already gone."

When no cars were coming, Cam, Eric, and Mr. Jansen crossed the street.

Cam shook her head. "They couldn't take it because a wedding cake is too tall to fit in their cars."

They walked toward Ken's truck.

"Do you know who did steal the cake?" Eric asked.

"Maybe," Cam said. "I just have to check one of the clues."

Cam stopped near the front of Ken's truck. She bent and looked at the grass and street by the side of the truck.

"What are you looking for?" Eric asked.

"Cookie crumbs."

"Bob already found lots of crumbs."

"I know that," Cam said. "But I need to know where he found them."

Cam ran her fingers through the grass. She carefully checked the curb and the gutter. Her dad and Eric helped her.

"No crumbs," Cam said. "Now let's look behind the truck."

Cam, Eric, and Mr. Jansen walked behind the truck. Cam ran her fingers through the grass and found lots of crumbs. Eric found a broken cookie on the curb. Mr. Jansen found crumbs in the gutter.

"Look," Eric told Cam. "There's a trail of crumbs all the way to your dad's car."

Cam followed the trail of crumbs to her dad's car. But the trail didn't stop. It went along the side of the car and past it. It continued to the next car.

Cam followed the crumbs past Officer Davis, Ken, and Lucy.

"That's it!" Cam said when she got to the end of the trail. "Now I know who stole Ken's wedding cake."

Chapter Seven

"Who stole the cake?" Eric asked. "Do you think he ate it all? Did he eat the pastries and cookies, too?"

"That's too much for any one person to eat," Mr. Jansen said. "He must have shared it, or maybe he was having a party."

"Officer Davis," Cam said. "I have to tell you something."

The police officer closed her police pad. She turned.

"I know who stole the cake," Cam told her. "It was Mr. Fancy."

"Who is Mr. Fancy?" Officer Davis asked. "And did you see him take the cake?"

"I didn't see him. I don't even know what he looks like, but I know he did it."

Officer Davis shook her head and asked, "How could you know he's the thief if you never saw him?"

She turned away from Cam.

"Here comes my partner," she said to Ken and Lucy. "Maybe he spoke with someone who saw the cake being taken."

Officer Oppen, Bob, Danny, and Beth had just crossed the street. They were walking toward Officer Davis.

"Who is Mr. Fancy?" Eric whispered. "And how do you know he took the cake?"

"Tell me, too," her father said.

Cam walked a few steps away from Officer Davis. Eric and Mr. Jansen followed her.

"We know three things," Cam told them. "Someone saw the keys in the back door of Ken's truck. To see them, he had to be standing behind the truck."

Eric said, "Lots of people may have walked past the truck."

"Because of the trail of crumbs," Cam said, "we also know which way the thief went with the stolen pastries, cookies, and cake. He carried them from Ken's truck and past Dad's car."

Cam smiled.

"Dad," she said. "You gave me the third clue, and it's very important."

"I did?"

"You reminded me that wedding cakes are tall, that Ken needs a truck with a roof high enough to hold them."

"Mom and I had a really tall cake at our wedding. We held hands and cut the first few pieces together."

Mr. Jansen smiled.

"She put a small piece of cake on her fork and fed it to me. Then I put a small piece on my fork and fed it to her."

"Would your cake have fit in the back of a car?" Eric asked.

"No," Mr. Jansen said, shaking his head.

"There was a yellow truck parked right behind your car," Cam said. "'Mr. Fancy Fix-It' was printed on the side of the truck."

"That's it!" Eric said. "When Mr. Fancy went to his truck, he must have seen Ken's keys. Then he must have opened the back door of Ken's truck. He saw the cake, cookies, and pastries and took them. He has a truck, so he had room for the wedding cake."

"He was in a hurry because he didn't want

to get caught," Mr. Jansen said. "That's why he dropped cookies. That's why he left a trail of crumbs."

Mr. Jansen thought for a moment.

"You didn't prove Mr. Fancy is the thief," he said. "But all those clues do point a finger at him."

"I think he did it," Eric said. "Let's tell the police."

Mr. Jansen went to Officer Oppen and said, "My daughter may know who took the cakes."

Officer Oppen asked Cam, "Did you remember something? Do you have a picture in your mental camera of something you saw?"

"I remembered clues," Cam said.

She told him the same clues she had told her father and Eric.

"Listen to this," Officer Oppen told his partner. "I think the *'Click! Click!'* girl found the thief."

Officer Davis, Lucy Lane, Ken the baker, Danny, Beth, and Old Bob listened as Cam

told them why she thought Mr. Fancy was the thief.

"I may know how to find him," Lucy Lane said. "I think I have a picture of his truck."

She looked at the back of her camera. She pushed a button and looked at the pictures she had taken.

"Look! Here's a picture of Ken. Behind him is Mr. Fancy's truck. It's yellow."

Officers Oppen and Davis looked at the picture.

"It would really help," Officer Davis said,

"if you had a picture of the truck's license plate. Then we could find out who Mr. Fancy is. I don't think that's his real name."

"I have pictures, too," Cam said. "They're in my head."

Cam closed her eyes. She said, *"Click!"* She said, *"Click!"* again.

"Here it is! I found it! It's a yellow truck. MR. FANCY FIX-IT, NO JOB TOO BIG OR TOO SMALL is printed on the side of the truck. There's also a telephone number and an e-mail address."

Cam told the officers the number and the address.

Officer Davis said, "That might be all we need to find Mr. Fancy. We can check his truck and see if he took the cake."

"Could you please hurry?" Ken asked. "It's almost time for the wedding to start."

Chapter Eight

Officer Davis took out her cell phone. She called the police station and reported the information Cam had given her about Mr. Fancy's truck.

"I'm sure we'll find him," Officer Oppen said. "If he stole your desserts, we'll find those, too."

"I'll call if I have any news," Officer Davis told Ken. "I have your cell phone number."

The two police officers walked to their car. They got in and drove off.

"I'm going to the wedding," Lucy Lane said. "It's almost time for me to start taking pictures."

"What about me?" Ken asked. "The bride and groom will want to see their cake."

Ken took out his cell phone.

"Oh, please," he told his phone. "Ring now. Ring with good news."

"I'll take my pictures," Lucy said. "That will keep everyone busy for a while. When I'm done, I'll call you. Maybe by then you'll have good news. If not, you'll have to come and tell the bride and groom about their cake."

Lucy Lane got in her car and drove off.

Ken stood by his truck. He held his cell phone and waited.

"We should go back inside," Mr. Jansen told Cam, Eric, Danny, Beth, and Bob. "We should finish the talent show."

"I want to see you juggle," Old Bob told Eric and Beth.

Cam, her father, her friends, and Bob went into the senior center. The seniors were in the main hall. Many were sitting and talking. Others were standing by the tables eating cake and fruit and drinking ice tea and water.

Mr. Jansen got up on the stage. He tapped on the microphone.

"Hello again," he said. "I'm sure you'll be happy to know that my daughter Jennifer may have found the thief. Hopefully, Ken will soon have his wedding cake. Now, if you will all be seated, we will continue with the Fall talent show."

Seniors standing by the tables found seats.

Cam sat by the window and watched Ken.

Danny stood by the stage.

"I can tell more jokes," he whispered to Mr. Jansen.

"I'm sorry, Danny," Mr. Jansen said, "but you had your turn."

"Here's a good joke," Danny said. "What would you do if you broke your leg in two places?"

"I'm happy once again," Mr. Jansen said into the microphone, "to call up two great jugglers, Eric Shelton and Beth Kane."

"If I broke my leg in two places," Danny

told Mr. Jansen, "I would just stop going to those places."

"Please, sit down," Mr. Jansen told him.

Eric and Beth walked toward the stage. Danny walked to an empty seat. He sat down.

Crunch!

"Oh, no!" Danny called out. "I sat on the cookies in my pockets."

Danny reached into his back pocket. He took out a handful of cookie crumbs and chocolate chips. As he ate them, lots of the crumbs stuck to his cheeks and chin.

"Look," Cam said, and pointed out the window. "Ken is talking on his cell phone. I'll bet the police called him. I'll bet they found Mr. Fancy."

Cam ran outside. Lots of people followed her.

"They found Mr. Fancy!" Ken told them. "All the desserts were still in his truck. They're coming here. I'll be able to get to the wedding before it starts."

Ken looked at Cam.

"You did it. You saved my cake."

"Bob, my dad, and Eric helped," Cam said.

"As a reward," Ken told her, "I'm going to bake a wedding cake just for you and your friends."

"I'm only ten," Cam said, laughing. "I'm too young to get married."

Ken laughed. "I meant I'll bake you a birthday cake."

"Cam's birthday is May fourth," Mr. Jansen said.

"That's not for a long time. Why don't you just come to my bakery? I'll give you lots of delicious breads, muffins, and cookies."

Bob said, "I'll also give you a reward. You and your friends can come to my store, Old Bob's Mystery Bookshop. Each of you can pick out a book."

A police car drove up. Behind it were a yellow truck and another police car. Officer Oppen got out of the yellow truck. He opened the two back doors of the truck. Ken looked in.

"There they are," Ken said. "The wedding cake and the trays of pastries and cookies."

Officer Davis got out of her car. She opened the back door and a man got out. His hands were locked in handcuffs. Two other police officers got out of the second car.

"This is Mr. Fancy," Officer Davis told Ken. "His real name is Mr. Bailor and he took your cakes."

Mr. Bailor's head was down.

"I'm sorry," he mumbled.

"We have to hurry," Ken said. "We have to move the cake into my truck and get it to the wedding."

"Why do you have to move the cake?" Mr. Jansen asked. "Why don't you just take it to the wedding in Mr. Fancy's truck?"

"I'll drive," Officer Oppen said.

"We'll follow you," Officer Davis and the two other police officers said.

"Wow!" Ken said. "My cake will get a police escort to the wedding. I bet the bride and groom and all their guests will be surprised when I drive up."

Everyone watched as the yellow truck, the two police cars, and Ken's truck drove off.

Bob said, "That was so exciting."

"Let's go back in," Mr. Jansen said. "Maybe now Eric and Beth can finally do their juggling act."

"Yeah," Danny said. "And I can finally eat some cookies that aren't broken."

"Wait," Cam said. "Let me take one more picture of all my friends."

Everyone stopped. They turned and faced Cam.

"Wipe your face," Beth whispered to Danny. "It's covered with cookie crumbs."

Danny wiped the crumbs off.

Mr. Jansen smiled. He was so proud of his daughter. The others smiled, too.

Cam blinked her eyes and said, *"Click!"*

A Cam Jansen Memory Game

Take another look at the picture opposite page 1. Study it. Blink your eyes and say, *"Click!"* Then turn back here and answer the questions at the bottom of the page. Please, first study the picture, *then* look at the questions.

1. Who are the two people sitting in the front seat of the car?

2. Is Cam wearing a seatbelt?

3. How many children are sitting in the backseat?

4. How many cars are in the picture?

5. How many houses are in the picture?

6. Does Mr. Jansen have both his hands on the steering wheel?